Shadow of Faith

PRAISE FOR *STORYSHARES*

"One of the brightest innovators and game-changers in the education industry."
– Forbes

"Your success in applying research-validated practices to promote literacy serves as a valuable model for other organizations seeking to create evidence-based literacy programs."

- Library of Congress

"We need powerful social and educational innovation, and Storyshares is breaking new ground. The organization addresses critical problems facing our students and teachers. I am excited about the strategies it brings to the collective work of making sure every student has an equal chance in life."
– Teach For America

"Around the world, this is one of the up-and-coming trailblazers changing the landscape of literacy and education."
- International Literacy Association

"It's the perfect idea. There's really nothing like this. I mean wow, this will be a wonderful experience for young people."   - Andrea Davis Pinkney, Executive Director, Scholastic

"Reading for meaning opens opportunities for a lifetime of learning. Providing emerging readers with engaging texts that are designed to offer both challenges and support for each individual will improve their lives for years to come. Storyshares is a wonderful start."
- David Rose, Co-founder of CAST & UDL

Shadow of Faith

Sara Hashem

STORYSHARES

Story Share, Inc.
New York. Boston. Philadelphia.

Storyshares
Story Share, Inc.
24 N. Bryn Mawr Avenue #340
Bryn Mawr, PA 19010-3304
www.storyshares.org

Inspiring reading with a new kind of book.

Interest Level: Middle School
Grade Level Equivalent: 3.4

9781642613179

Book design by Storyshares

Printed in the United States of America

Storyshares Presents

1

"Do you, like, shower with it on?"

I sigh. "No. It's made of cloth. I only wear it around men I'm not related to."

"So, your dad can see your hair?" Matt asks.

I nod.

"Can I see it?"

"No, Matt, you can't."

Before Matt can convince me to give him a peek, Mina swoops to my rescue, finally finished with her chemistry class. "Dude, beat it!" she tells Matt. "It's a hijab, not a museum exhibit."

Matt rolls his eyes. "Whatever. Bet your hair isn't even that great."

At Mina's murderous glare, he quickly leaves our secluded corner of the noisy high school. We unwrap our lunches on the rickety table. Mina has her phone out, undoubtedly texting her latest crush. When she sees me pull a book from my backpack, she stops me. "Don't even think about it."

"How come you can text and I can't read?"

"Texting takes a second. When you read, you vanish for ages. There, see, no more texting." She tosses her phone into her bag and waits.

Reluctantly, I put my book away and turn my attention to the turkey sandwich I'd made this morning. Mina chatters about the latest trend sweeping the school.

Something about black skinny jeans and high tops. "The Kardashians can wear them, but I definitely can't.

Have you seen my butt? No way can I pull those off."

I take a bite of my sandwich and wait for her to pause before offering my opinion. "I think you look great in your normal pants."

"Samar, I love you, but you're not really a fashion expert." She glances meaningfully at my slacks.

I frown. "What's that supposed to mean? These are comfortable."

"You look like a middle-aged lawyer."

I smooth my hands over my legs and shrug off Mina's remark. I've only been back in America for three months, but I've grown used to her little comments. The only reason I tolerate them is because I know she doesn't mean any harm. Unlike the Egyptian students I'd spent the last two years with, American kids are shockingly impolite.

My father had moved my family to Egypt after I finished the sixth grade. It wasn't a real surprise, although it had caused friction between my parents. Both were Egyptian, but only my father felt ties to his homeland. In the short two years I'd spent there, I'd donned the hijab and met more family than I knew I had.

When Arab Spring broke out and it was obvious we would have to return to California, I hadn't known how to feel. I was glad to go back to America: I spoke the language perfectly and understood the ins and outs of the educational system. But on the other hand, I wasn't prepared to lose the love and warmth I'd gotten used to in Egypt.

Mina had tried to absorb me into her friend group when I'd returned, but it was no use. I simply couldn't sit at the table and listen to their petty whining. Instead of listening, I'd wonder whether the state-wide curfew in Egypt had been lifted, or if my friends were safe at our old school.

Though I'm grateful for Mina's friendship, and her efforts to help me socialize, I can't decide where I belong.

2

As I get up to toss my lunch away, I bump into Faith Jackson. "Sorry," I say automatically, stepping back. She flashes me a tight smile, throws out her lunch, and hurries back to her table.

"Ugh, she's so rude," Mina snaps when I return to my seat.

I arch a brow. "For throwing away her lunch?"

"She didn't even apologize. Or acknowledge you."

"I think you're making too much of it."

Mina leans in and says quietly, "You know she's Christian, right?"

"Uh, most of the school is."

"Yeah, but she's one of *those* Christians. Evangelical. The psycho ones."

I make a mental note to research "Evangelical" later, but I don't want to appear even more out of the loop with Mina, so I shrug. The bell rings, and I hastily make my goodbyes before darting off to Spanish.

Taking my normal seat at the back of the class, I extract my book and flip to where I'd left off. I'm only halfway a page when I hear the question I always dread: "What book is that?"

I look up and freeze. It's Faith Jackson. She has turned around in her seat, directly in front of me, and is waiting for my answer. I'm astounded. We've both sat here the last three months, and I can't remember her ever talking to me.

"Um, it's a romance. Fantasy, too."

"Can I see the cover? Maybe I've read it."

I mechanically lift the book and wince, waiting for the flash of judgment to pass over her eyes. I doubt that the boy and girl gazing longingly at each other on the cover appeal to her Christian values. They don't appeal to my Muslim ones, either.

Faith brightens. "Hey! That's on my to-read shelf. Is it any good?"

We make small talk about the book. I try not to sound robotic or wooden, but it's difficult. I'm afraid of saying the wrong thing, of seeing the psycho Christian side of Faith that Mina warned me about.

But if the psycho is there, I never see it. Mr. Monroe starts class, and Faith shoots me a friendly smile before turning to the front of the room. I put away my book and wonder whether or not to tell Mina about this conversation. I ultimately decide against it. I may not know much about the pants the Kardashians wear, but I do know how to read people, and something about Faith Jackson makes me want to flip the page.

3

I lie to Mina and have lunch in the locker room the next day. The turkey sandwich I'd made lies untouched on the wooden bench. I force back the tears I'd been fighting since last night.

Mom had insisted on taking my siblings and me to the mosque every family night, no matter how many times I begged to be left at home. I loved going to the prayer room, absorbing the peaceful environment of people reading the Quran, and lifting my hands to make my own prayers.

What I hated was the youth group. Everyone knew each other, and they tried to include me. But I didn't understand their references, and I wasn't interested in their drama. I felt more uncomfortable with them than I did with Mina's friend group. At least Mina's friends just mocked me for being an out-of-place teenager. At the mosque, however, their mockery targeted my Islam, and that was worse than any comment about my pants.

A sound at the door of the locker room captures my attention. I wipe under my eyes as Faith enters, gym bag in hand. Quickly glancing at my sandwich, I debate whether to say hi or to pretend we're strangers.

She takes the matter out of my hands. "Are you okay?"

To my horror, a rush of tears overwhelms me. They stream down my cheeks, and I cover my face. "I'm f-f-fine," I stammer.

I hear a shuffling. Peeking between my fingers, I see Faith move my sandwich aside and straddle the bench in front of me. She waits until I've calmed down.

"What happened? Something with Mina?" she asks.

I shake my head. "It's not important. Sorry, I'm a mess."

"We've all been there. Heck, I was on this bench crying last week. They really should build a separate room for emotional cry-fests, don't you think?"

I'm intrigued by the first personal piece of information she's shared. "Why were you crying? If you don't mind my asking," I say.

Laughing lightly, she tucks a strand of hair behind her ear and blushes. "It's stupid."

"I'll tell you if you tell me," I offer.

"Boy, you're stubborn," Faith says. "I thought you were supposed to be shy."

"I'm not shy. Just quiet."

She nods slowly. "I didn't think of it that way. Ok, you've got yourself a deal. Well, I was crying last week because we're moving. I'm not even switching schools or anything. It's only a few miles away, but I didn't want to leave the house I grew up in. See? Stupid."

"Not at all. Leaving your home can't be easy, regardless of where you're moving."

"I guess. I feel silly telling you this. Didn't you move here from Egypt?"

I blink. I didn't expect people to know anything about me other than that I'm the only kid at school who wears a scarf. "Yeah, but I lived here originally. I was only in Egypt for two years."

Faith seems interested. She props her chin on her hand. "So you not only moved out of your home, you moved out of the country. What was it like? I've never left California."

I glance at my watch. There's not enough time left of lunch to find the words to describe the rollercoaster that was my life in Egypt. "Wait!" Faith exclaims before I speak. "You never told me why you were crying. Fair is fair."

The bell rings before I can answer. I smirk at Faith, but she's not letting go easily. "We have Spanish together. We can walk and talk."

4

Faith and I gather our things and make our way out of the locker room as a flood of girls enter. It feels strange to walk with her. I notice a few people glance at us. I imagine we make for quite a bizarre picture: the introverted Muslim and the quirky Christian.

"I was crying because I have the social skills of a banana," I blurt. I think I startle Faith, because her laughter is loud and heartfelt. It's contagious, and I laugh, too.

"What makes you say that?" Faith asks me.

"Well, do you know what a mosque is?"

She hesitates. "Is that your guys' church?"

"Yeah, kind of. My Mom always makes us go during family night. I just can't bring myself to interact with my youth group. Yesterday they were discussing Queen Bee. I pitched in about my thoughts on pollen. I thought we were talking about actual bees, not Beyoncé."

Students turn to look at us as we enter Spanish, thanks to Faith's second explosion of laughter. She braces her hand on her desk and holds her stomach. I wait for her to finish, but another wave of amusement hits, and she's laughing all over again.

I take my seat. She drops her backpack on her desk and turns towards me, wiping her eyes. "That was the best thing I've heard all week."

"Glad to be of service," I chuckle.

Faith grins. "Good grief. You know, that actually happened to me at my church youth group. They were talking about some political event going on at the time. I thought it was the plot of the book we'd been assigned by our pastor. They listened to me ramble on about context and grammar for fifteen minutes before cluing me in."

I open my mouth to tease her, but the sudden silence of the class alerts me to Mr. Monroe. He's hovering over our desks, head tilted and brow furrowed. "Ladies. Am I going to have to separate you?"

Faith turns to the front of the room, and I shake my head. "No, sir."

"Good. Keep the noise level to a minimum, please."

I'm too embarrassed to do anything but stare at my notebook for the next twenty minutes. The doodles I'm scrawling are thrown off track when a folded piece of paper lands on my desk. I glance up, but there's nobody looking in my direction. I unravel the note and read it out of Mr. Monroe's sight.

This is my cell number. Text me later.

It's from Faith. I stare at the digits for a lot longer than I should before I stow it away in my notebook.

5

"I'm sorry, did you just say Faith Jackson is having lunch with us?" Mina asks on our way to the table. She'd thought I was joking the entire time I explained my budding friendship with Faith, and the lunch thing pushes her over the edge.

"Yes."

"Have you officially lost your mind, Samar? The chick is wacked!"

For some reason, the patience I usually exercise with Mina evaporates. "Stop saying that! How do you think it makes me feel that you immediately assume she's wacked just because she's religious?"

Mina's jaw drops. My outburst has taken her off guard. "I don't dislike her because she's religious, and you know I'd never think that about you."

"You might not, but other people probably do. I've seen the way people look at me, Mina. I'm not blind. I'd just appreciate it if we could avoid doing the same thing to others. What did she ever do to make you dislike her so much, anyway?"

Before Mina can reply, Faith appears at the table, lunch in hand and a hesitant smile on her face. "Hi," she says, looking at me for a cue.

"Hey, Faith. Take a seat," I say.

After a brief pause, Faith slides onto the bench.

"Hey, Mina. How's it going?"

Mina is sarcastic and rude, addressing her water when she says, "Just great, Faith. So happy you're joining us."

"Mina!" I burst out, but Faith lifts a hand to stop me.

"It's alright," she sighs. "I deserve that."

"No, you don't," I argue. "Mina, what's wrong with you?"

I jump when Mina slams her water bottle onto the table. I've never seen her so angry. "Why don't you ask your new best friend? I'm going to the bathroom." She leaves her lunch and practically runs to the restrooms, her long, dark brown hair flying in waves behind her.

I turn towards Faith. We had been texting nonstop the entire week and had nearly been separated in Spanish three times. I'm comfortable enough around her to feel that I deserve an explanation about what's going on between her and Mina.

Faith's eyes are shut tight. I think she's struggling not to cry. I pat her shoulder until she exhales and opens her eyes again. "Mina and I were best friends in middle school. I adored Mina, but I was having a really tough time at home. I turned to my church for comfort and support, to try to rebuild myself. But I'd lashed out at

Mina so many times. By the time I was okay again, she couldn't stand the sight of me. I can't blame her."

I have a dozen questions, but I settle on one. "What do you mean you lashed out?"

"She told me she had kissed Jenna Barclay at a spin-the-bottle party. I called her a....a....well, it was really terrible," Faith confesses, dropping her head into her hands. "I was so awful, Samar."

I wince in sympathy. I understood more than anyone what it's like to go through a period where change is the only thing you know. In moderation, change is wonderful, but when there's no stability to balance it out, it can become unpredictable and dangerous.

6

The next morning, Matt's constant torture takes a new turn. "Get off!" I swat Matt's hand away from my head. He's being more aggressive than usual. I'm in the hallway, waiting for Mina to get out of class. I start to wonder if I should wait somewhere else.

"Just let me see! I'm not going to fall in love with you when I look at your hair. I just want to take a quick look. Stop being so sensitive about it."

Matt reaches for me again. This time, I snatch my backpack and try to slide off my seat, but Matt grabs the back of my hijab and yanks. I gasp and fall back, hands flying to the pin at my throat. One of my arms snaps out, making contact with Matt's face. He curses and releases his hold. There's vengeance in his eyes when he moves towards me.

"Samar!" I hear Faith's voice, but it's too late. I claw uselessly at Matt's shirt, but he digs his fingers into my hijab and wrenches me to the side. The pin under my throat breaks, the sharp needle poking my skin. The other needles rip my hair, bringing tears to my eyes.

Suddenly, Matt is jerked away from me. Another pair of arms slides around my middle to keep me standing. The principal, Mr. Calloway, has Matt in an iron hold and is barking into his walkie-talkie, asking for the school nurse.

Mina chooses this moment to emerge from chemistry. She takes in the scene and rushes to my side.

"What happened?" she demands. "Oh my God, your throat is bleeding!"

I gently push Faith's arms off me and sit. I probe my throat cautiously. My fingers come away wet with little drops of blood. "It's not a big deal. The pin just pierced through the skin."

The school nurse and security guard burst through the double doors. The nurse shoots Matt a disgusted glance before heading towards me. She kneels down, observing my lopsided hijab and flushed face. Her gaze lands on my throat, as I knew it would.

"Honey, I'm going to have to ask you to take off the scarf," she says softly. "I need to see the laceration on your throat."

"It's fine. It barely even hurts," I assure her, but it doesn't work. She simply sits back and motions for me to remove my hijab. Ahead, I spot Matt watching me with a smirk. After all this, he's still going to get what he wanted. Tears fill my eyes, but I reach for my hijab.

"Wait," Faith says. She moves in front of the nurse and me, blocking us from Matt's view. She glances shyly at Mina and extends her hand. "Want to help?"

Mina bites her lip. She looks at Faith's hand for long enough that I begin to worry. But to my surprise, she heaves a sigh and laces her fingers with Faith's. Together, they form a wall in front of me, protecting me from Matt and anyone else who might walk by.

The tears that flow down my cheeks aren't sad this time. "Thank you, guys."

Mina glances over her shoulder and winks. "We've got your back, girl."

"Technically, your front," Faith corrects.

Groaning, Mina shakes her head. "You're so lame."

"This is true," Faith admits.

"Well, would you look at that? We finally agree on something."

About The Author

Sara Hashem is a contributing author to the Storyshares library.

About The Publisher

Story Shares is a nonprofit focused on supporting the millions of teens and adults who struggle with reading by creating a new shelf in the library specifically for them. The ever-growing collection features content that is compelling and culturally relevant for teens and adults, yet still readable at a range of lower reading levels.

Story Shares generates content by engaging deeply with writers, bringing together a community to create this new kind of book. With more intriguing and approachable stories to choose from, the teens and adults who have fallen behind are improving their skills and beginning to discover the joy of reading. For more information, visit storyshares.org.

Easy to Read. Hard to Put Down.

www.ingramcontent.com/pod-product-compliance
Lightning Source LLC
Chambersburg PA
CBHW071230170626
46809CB00005BA/2010

* 9 781642 613179 *